HOME, SWEET HOME

Everyone thinks they know the story of . . .

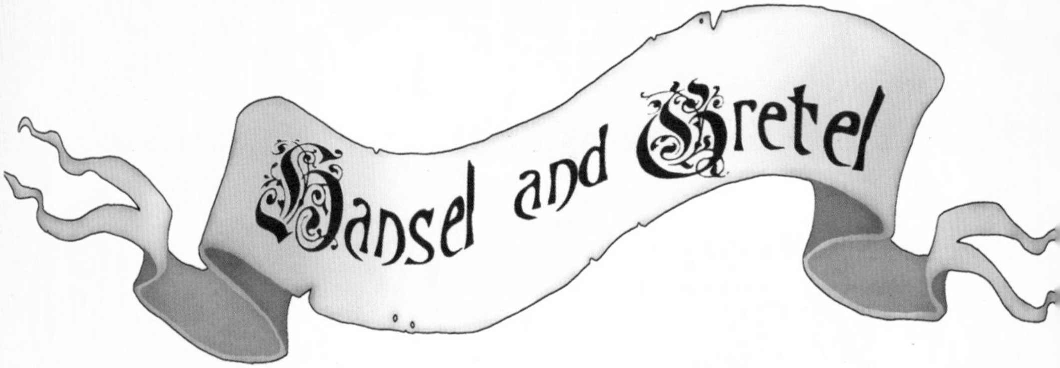
Hansel and Gretel

But here is the real story! First: I am not a witch!

And I did not want a candy house to catch children—this house was just the only one left!

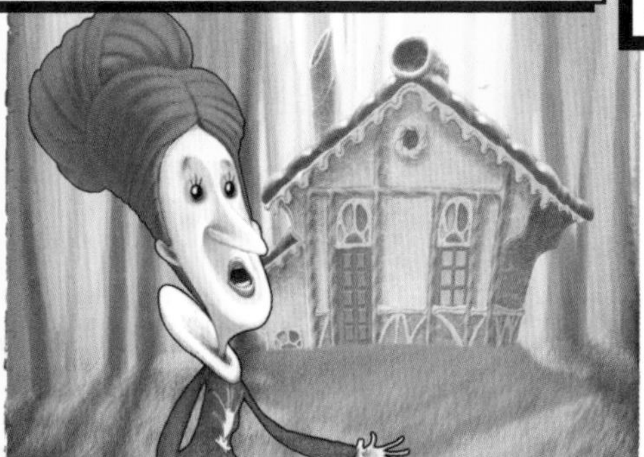

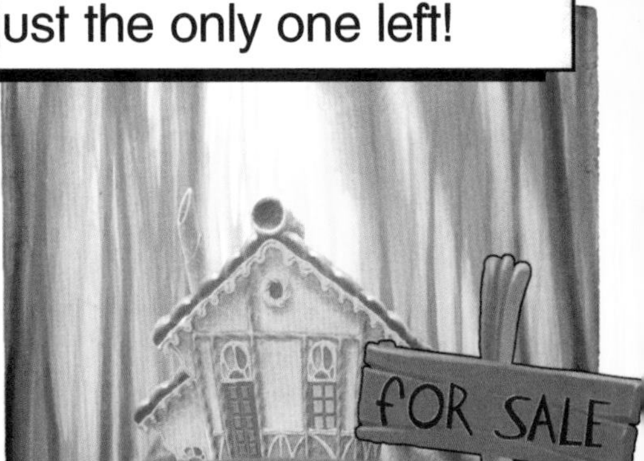
FOR SALE

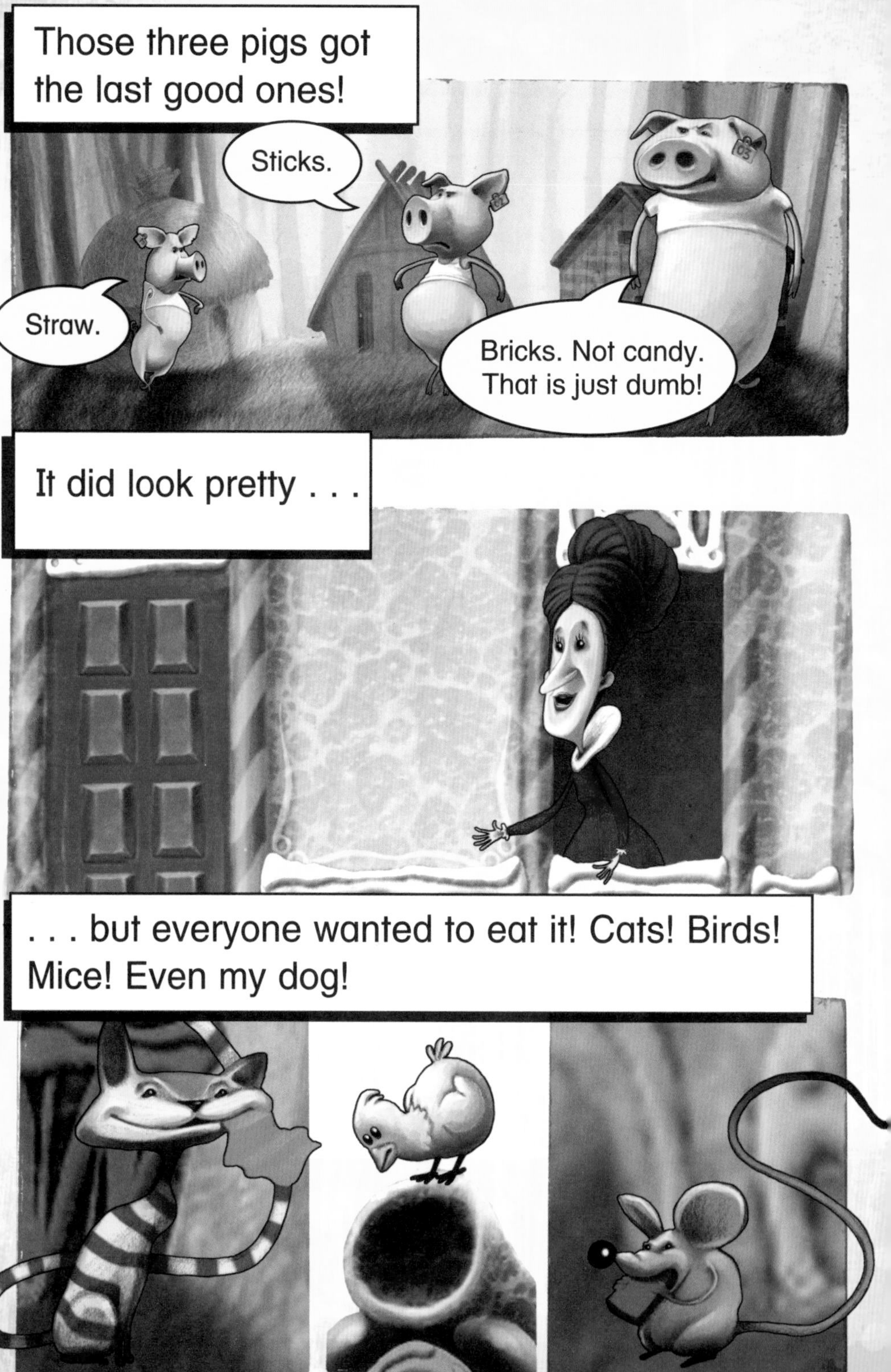
Those three pigs got the last good ones!
Straw.
Sticks.
Bricks. Not candy. That is just dumb!
It did look pretty . . .
. . . but everyone wanted to eat it! Cats! Birds! Mice! Even my dog!

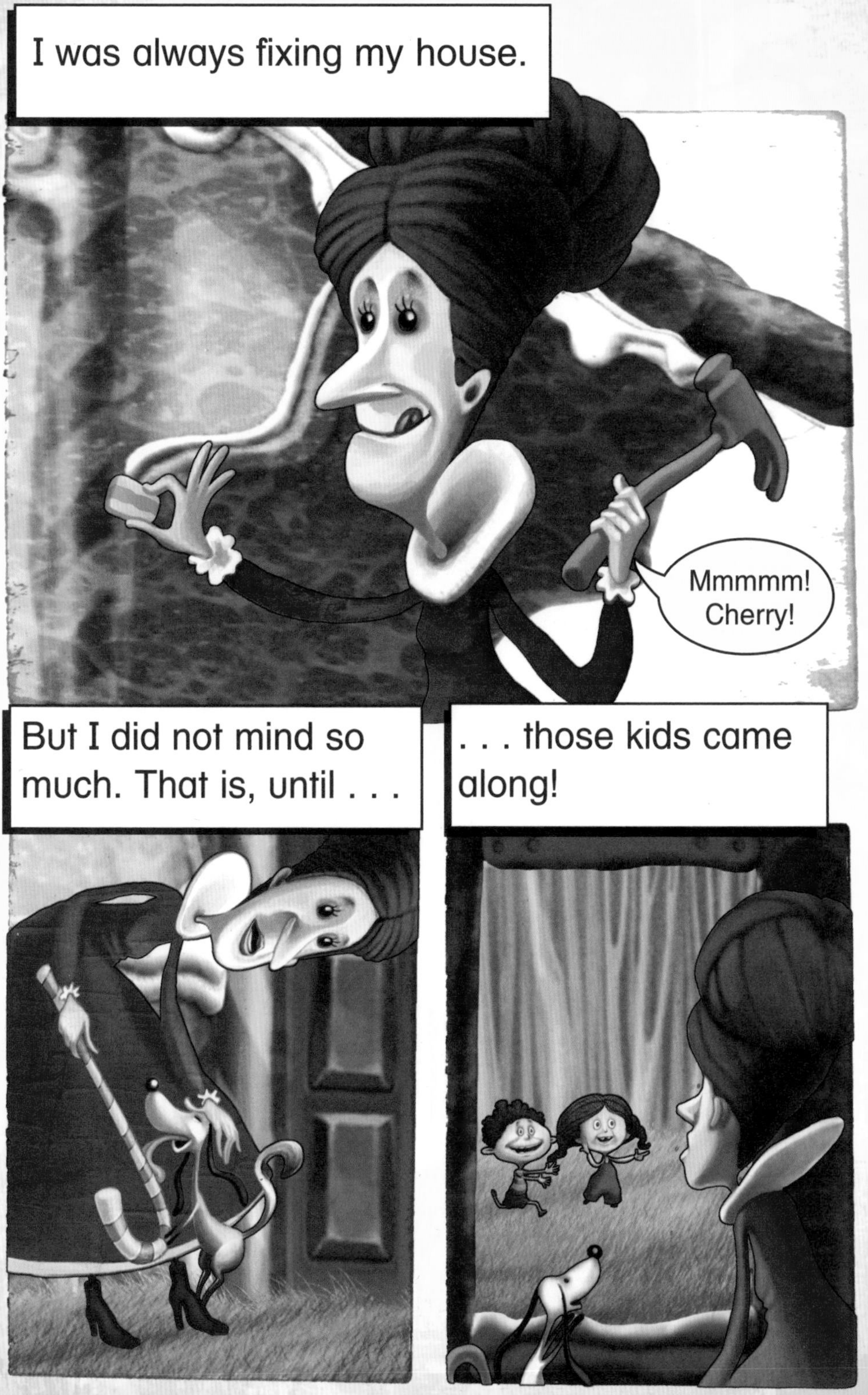
I was always fixing my house.
Mmmmm! Cherry!
But I did not mind so much. That is, until . . .
. . . those kids came along!

The story says they were left in the woods because their parents could not feed them.

I am sorry, children!

And that they ate my house because they were so hungry.

Ha! The truth is their parents would not let them eat sweets. So when they saw my house, they thought:

Dessert!

First, they ate the windows.

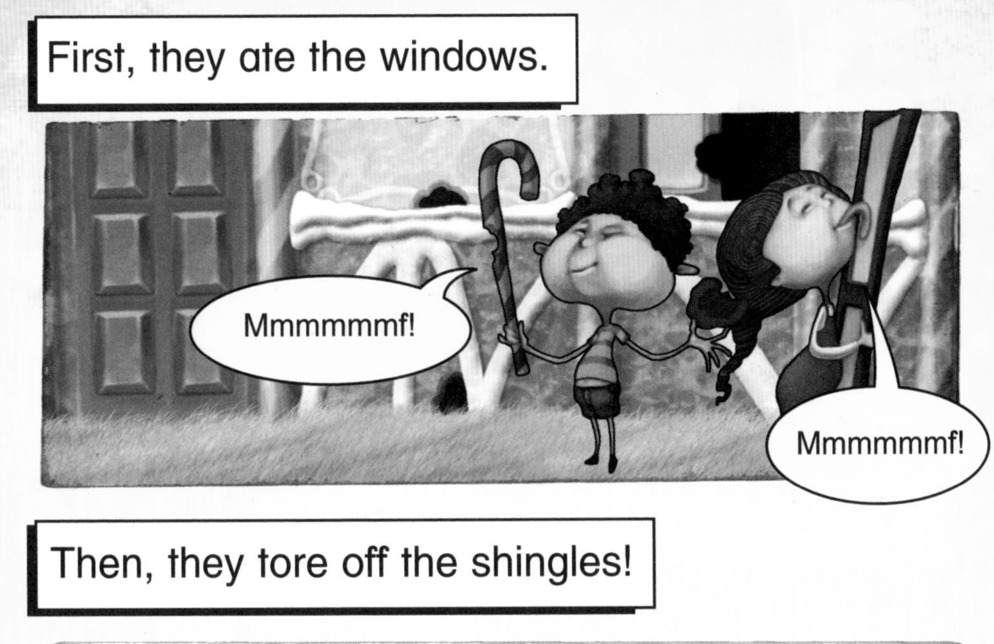
Mmmmmmf!
Mmmmmmf!

Then, they tore off the shingles!

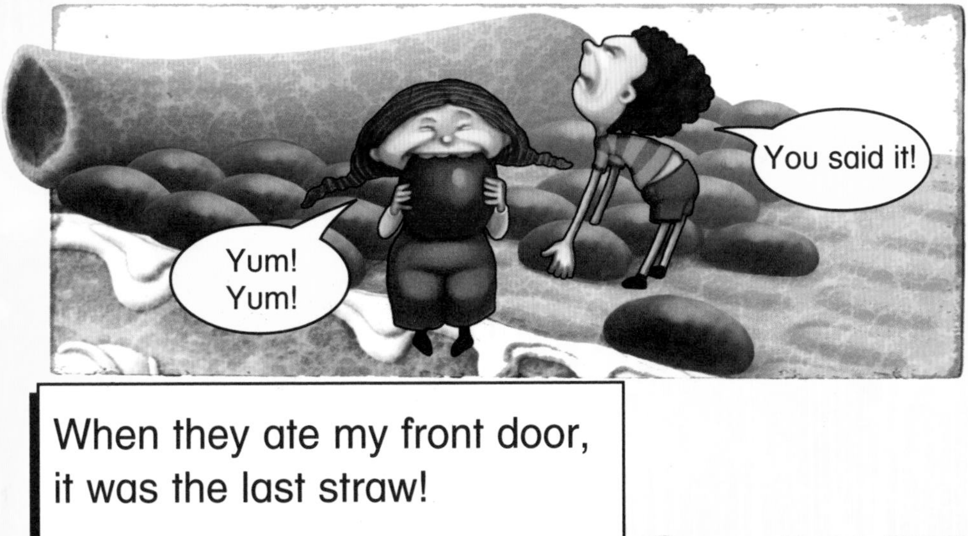
Yum!
Yum!
You said it!

When they ate my front door,
it was the last straw!

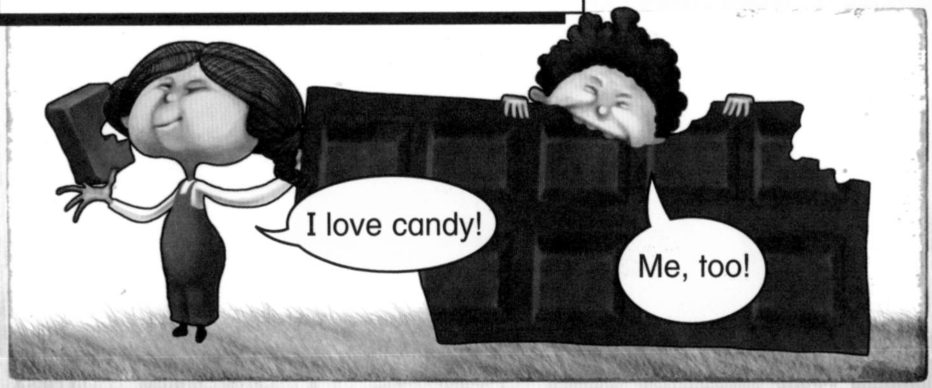
I love candy!
Me, too!

The story says I tried to fatten them up. Ha! They fattened themselves up!

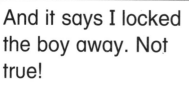

And it says I locked the boy away. Not true!

I locked them *both* away until their parents got there.

Time out!

Oh, dear.

We all learned a lesson that day.

Their parents learned it was okay to sometimes eat dessert.

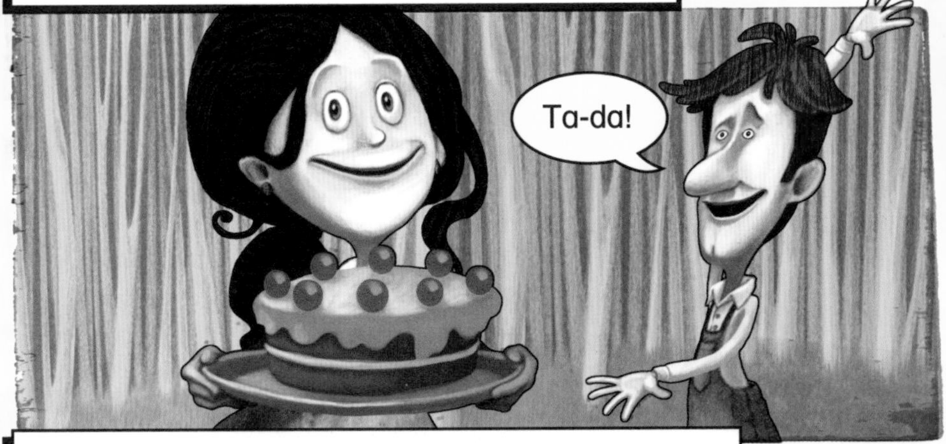
Ta-da!

The kids learned not to eat anyone's house without permission again.

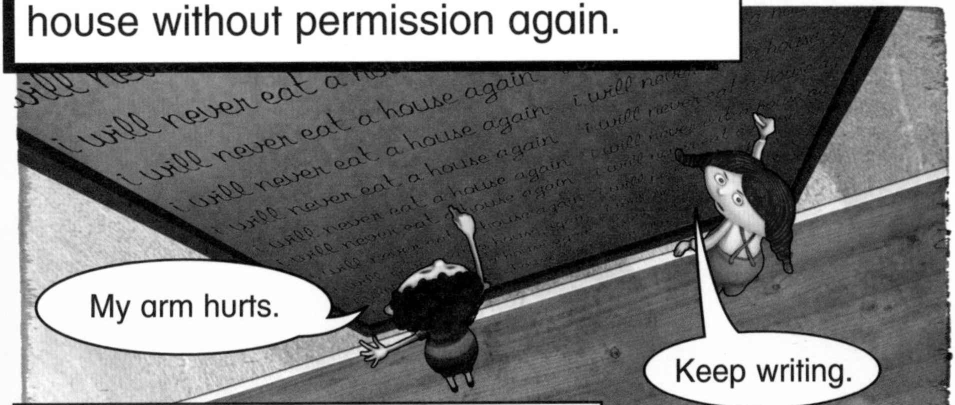
i will never eat a house again
i will never eat a house again
i will never eat a house again
i will never eat a house again
My arm hurts.
Keep writing.

And I learned to never, ever live in a house made of food!

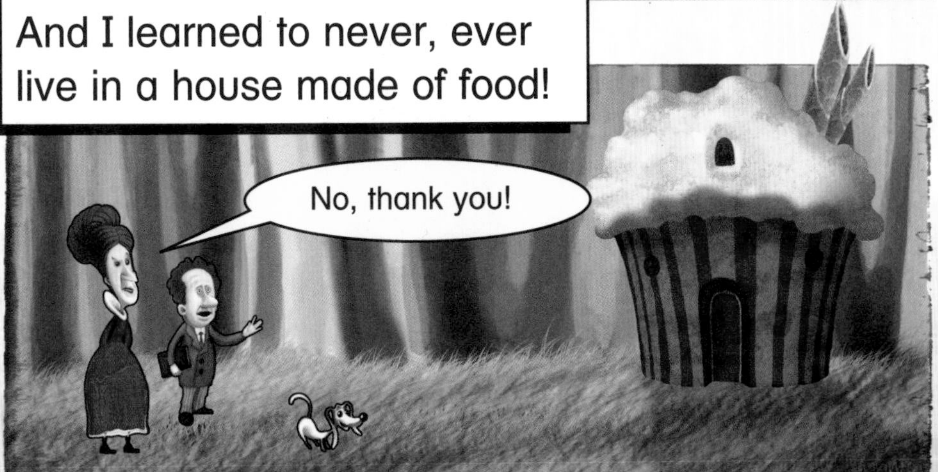
No, thank you!

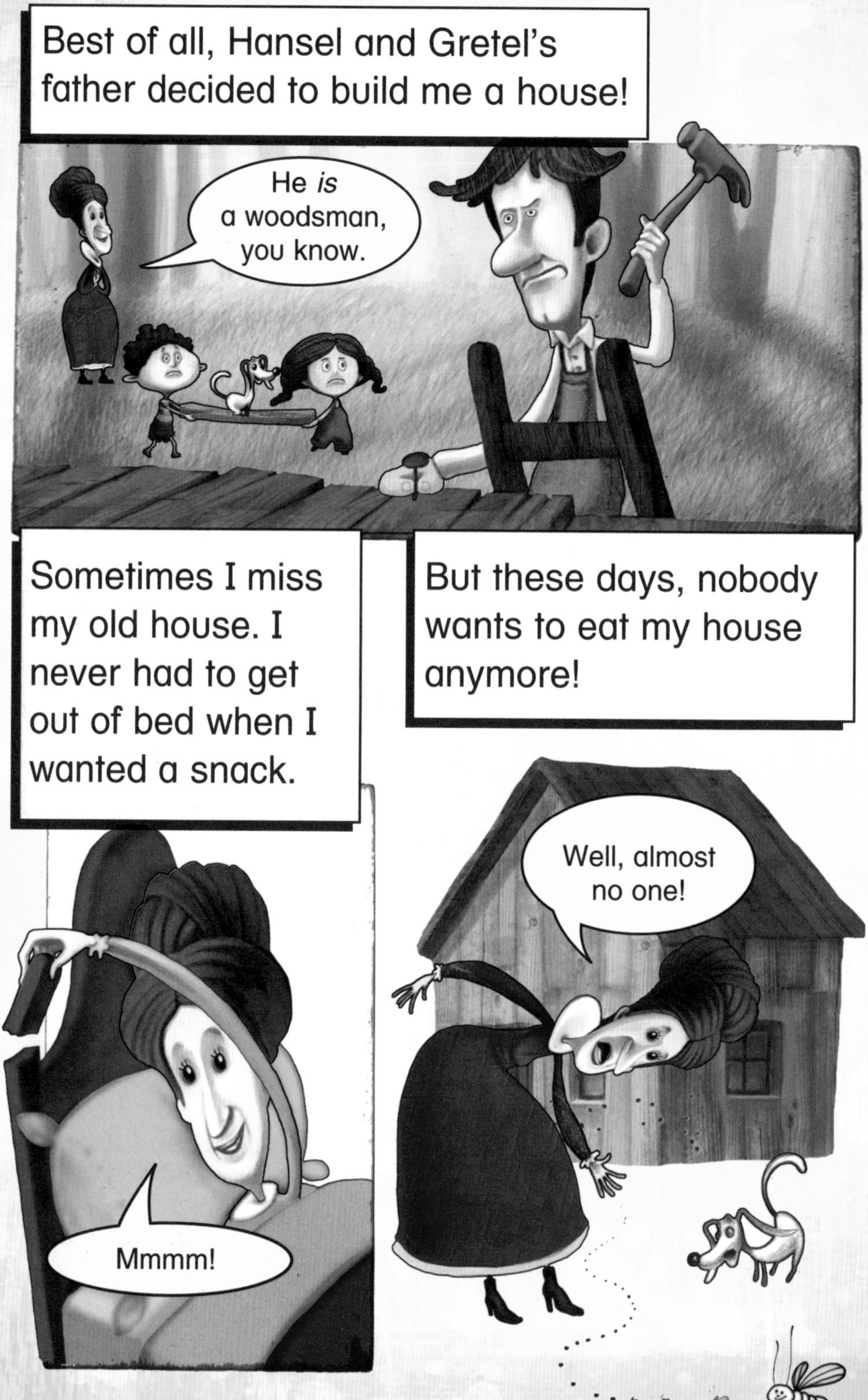
Best of all, Hansel and Gretel's father decided to build me a house!
He *is* a woodsman, you know.
Sometimes I miss my old house. I never had to get out of bed when I wanted a snack.
Mmmm!
But these days, nobody wants to eat my house anymore!
Well, almost no one!

BABYSITTER BLUES

Let me tell you the true story of . . .

Little Red Riding Hood

First of all, THIS did NOT happen:

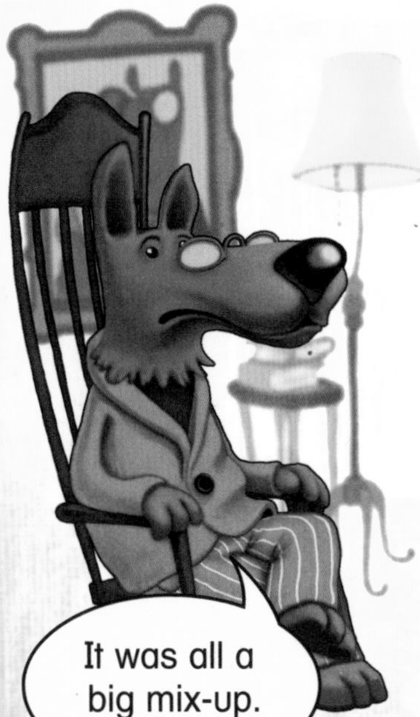
It was all a big mix-up.

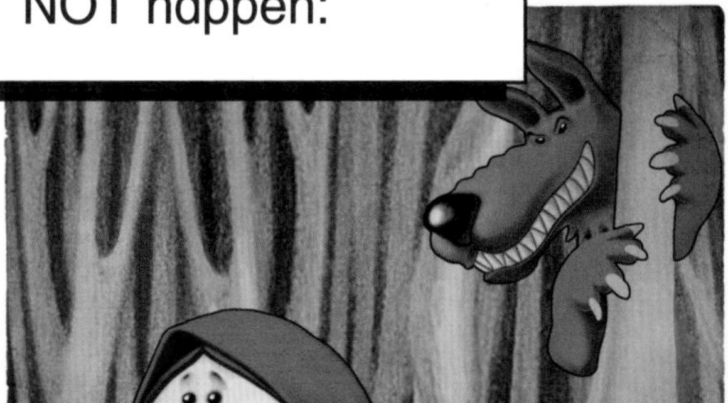

I was *asked* to come to her house.

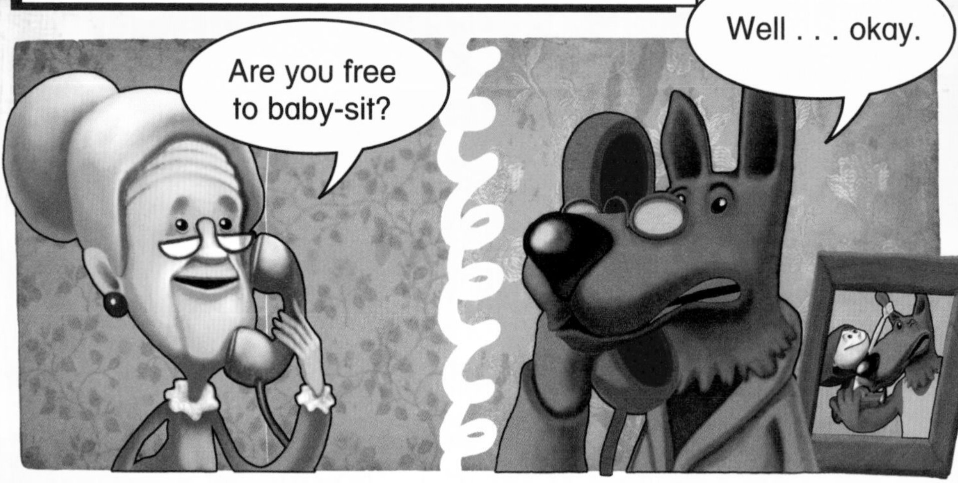
Are you free to baby-sit?
Well . . . okay.

Grandma had plans that night.

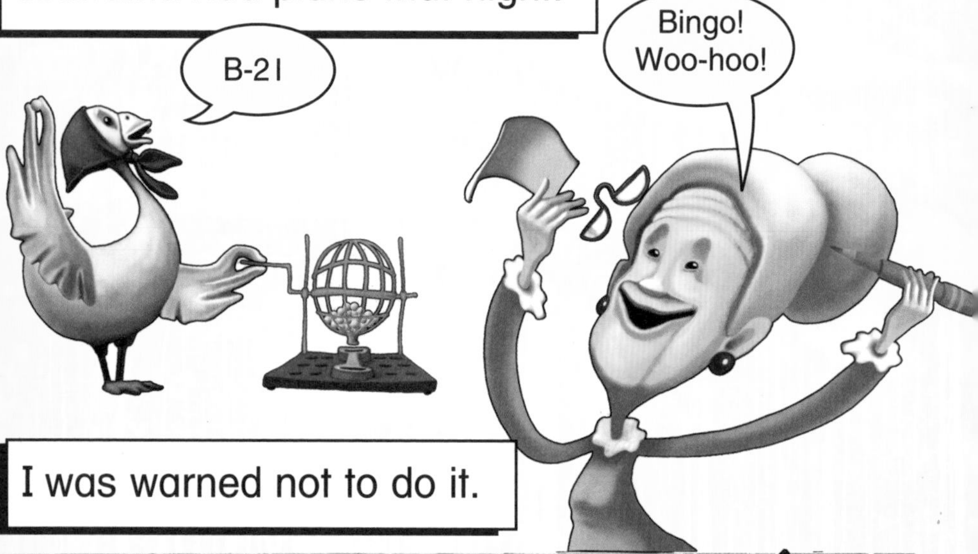
B-21
Bingo! Woo-hoo!

I was warned not to do it.

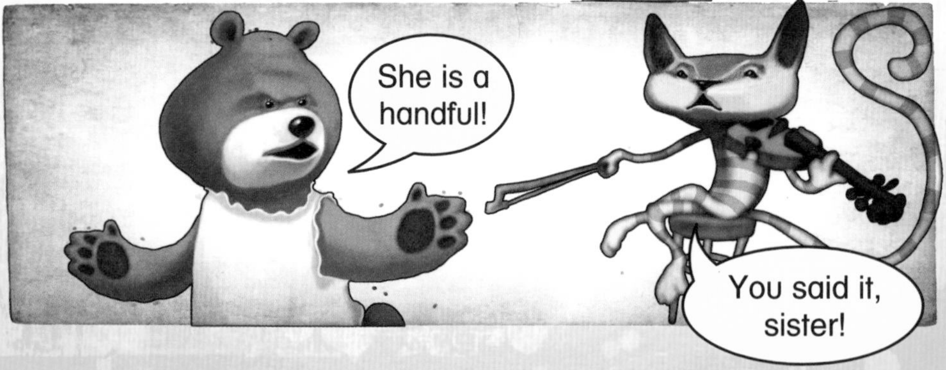
She is a handful!
You said it, sister!

But I knew I could handle it.

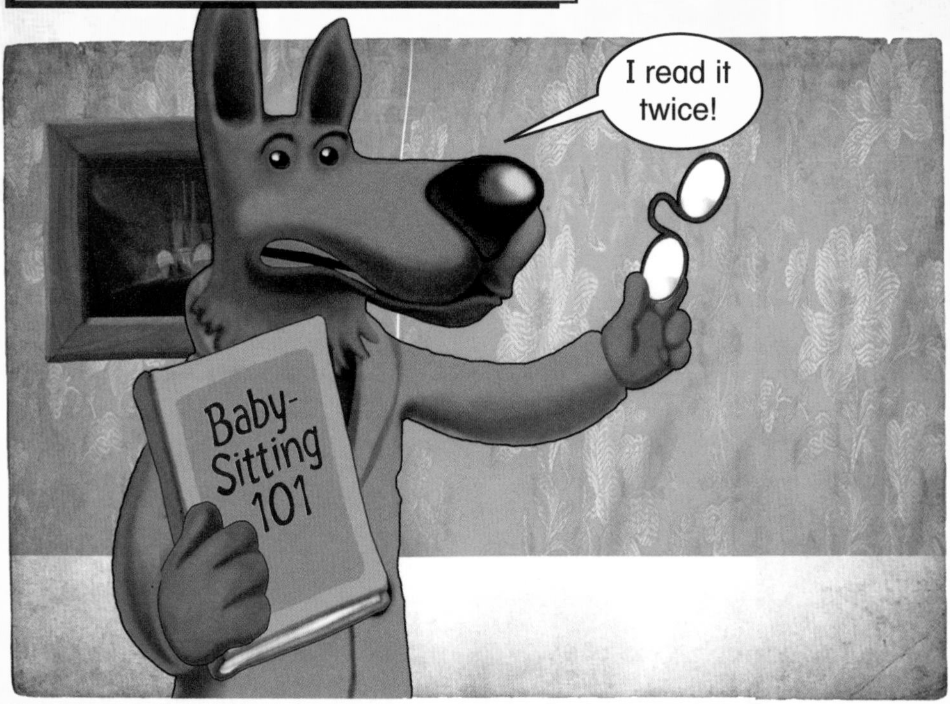
I read it twice!
Baby-Sitting 101

It started out okay. First we ate dinner.

Then we played some games.

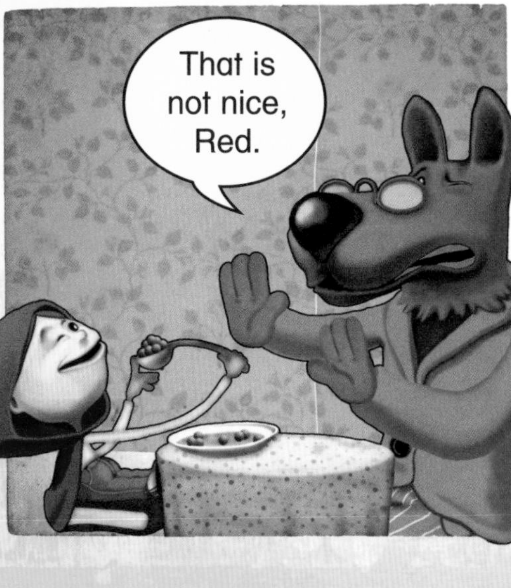
That is not nice, Red.

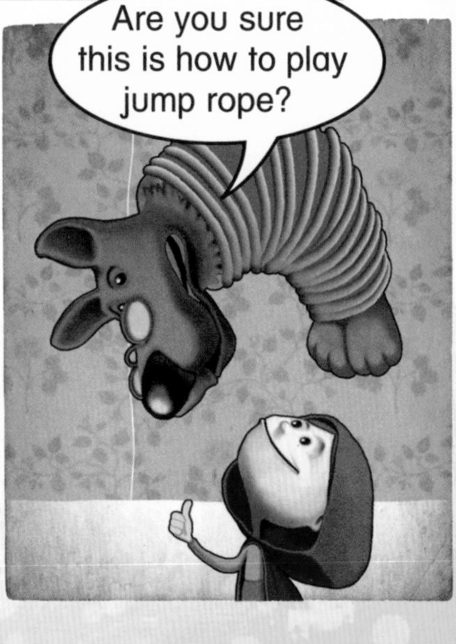
Are you sure this is how to play jump rope?

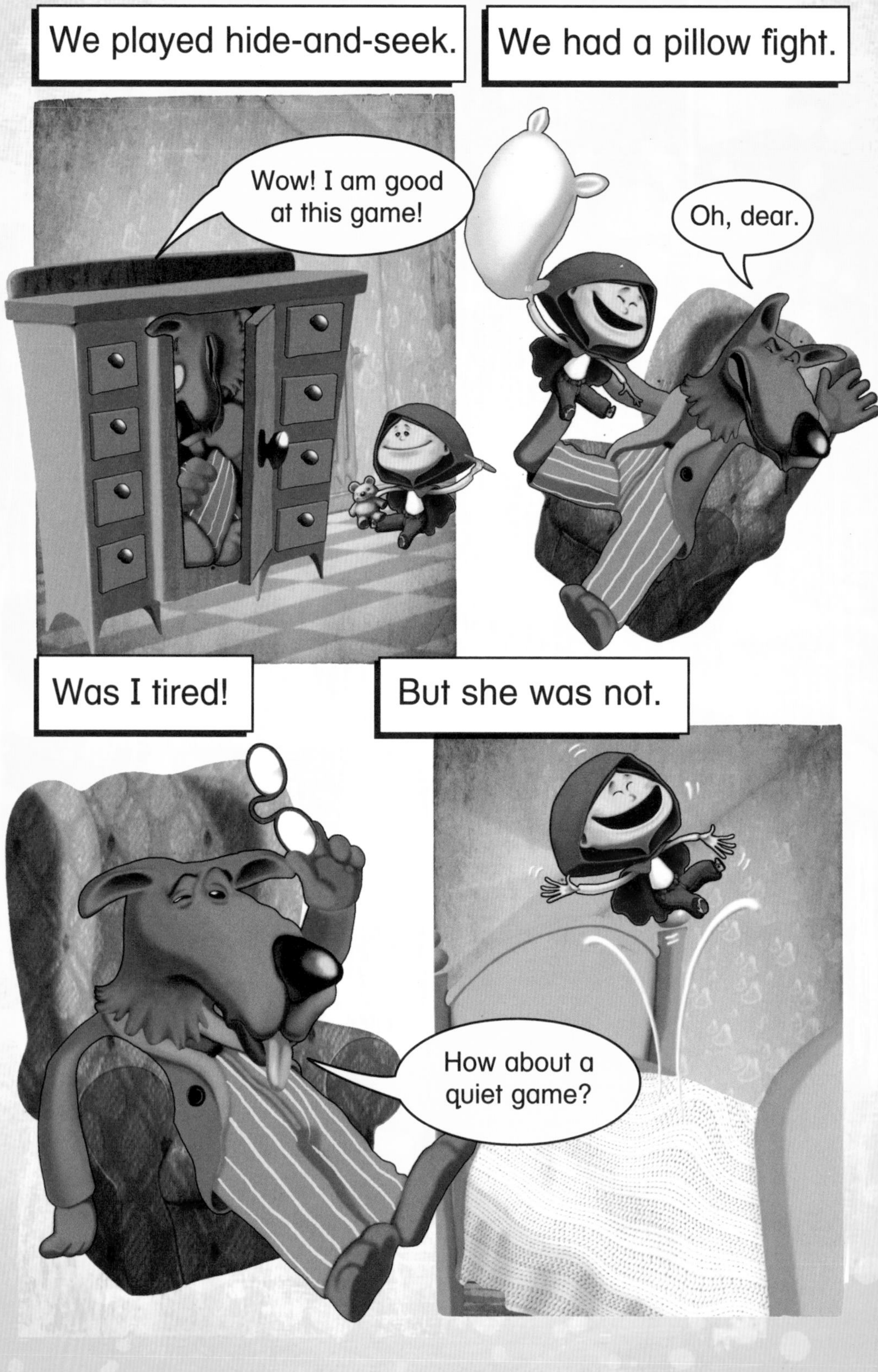
We played hide-and-seek.
Wow! I am good at this game!
We had a pillow fight.
Oh, dear.
Was I tired!
But she was not.
How about a quiet game?

Red had an idea. We would play dress-up!

You want me to wear what?

I was to pretend to be Grandma. So I got into bed and pulled the covers up to my chin.

Okay, I am ready.

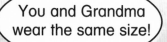

You and Grandma wear the same size!

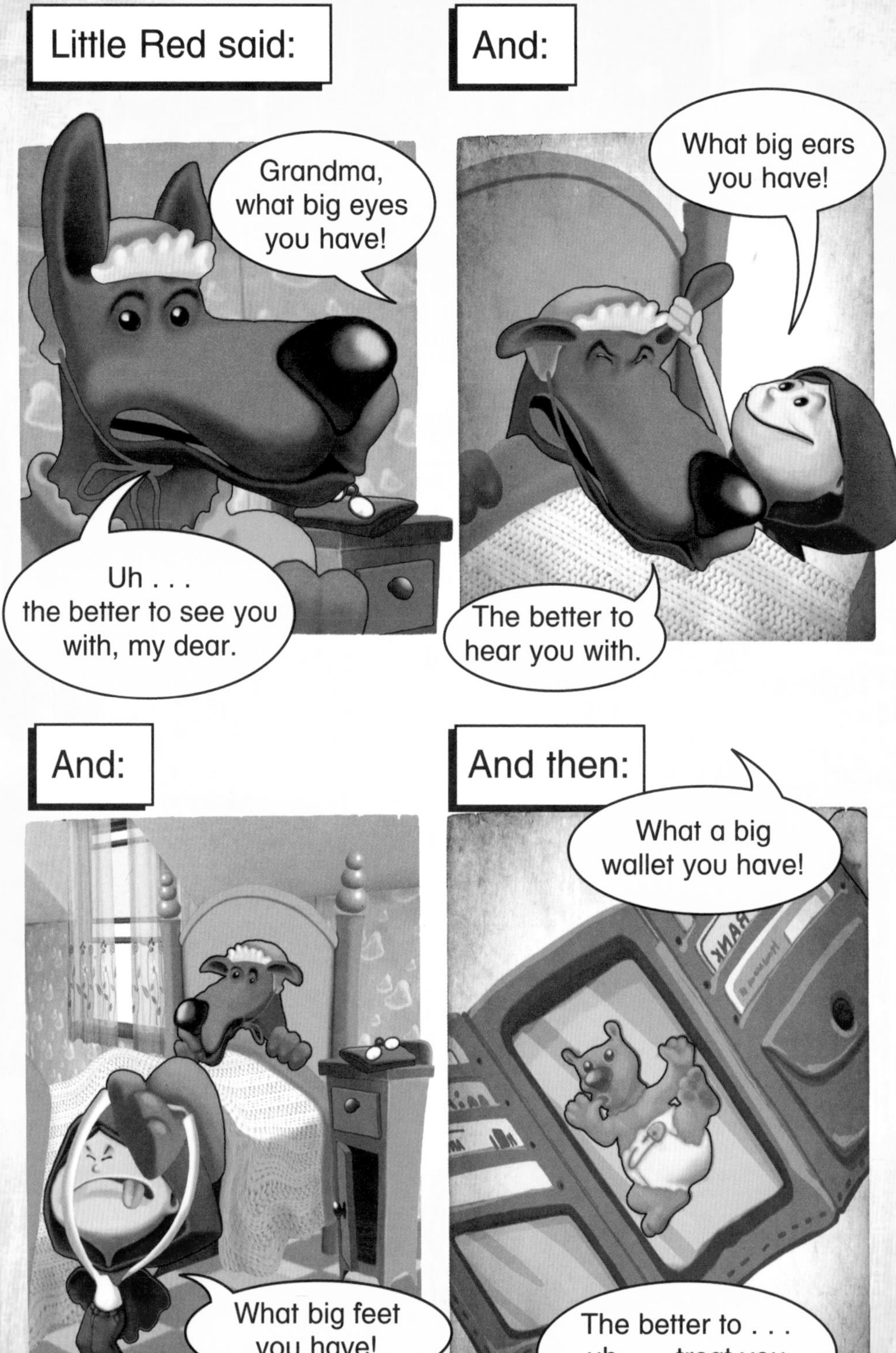
Little Red said:
Grandma, what big eyes you have!
Uh . . . the better to see you with, my dear.
And:
What big ears you have!
The better to hear you with.
And:
What big feet you have!
And then:
What a big wallet you have!
The better to . . . uh . . . treat you with!

This is when things went wrong. A passing woodsman heard me.

He thought I said, "The better to *eat* you with!"

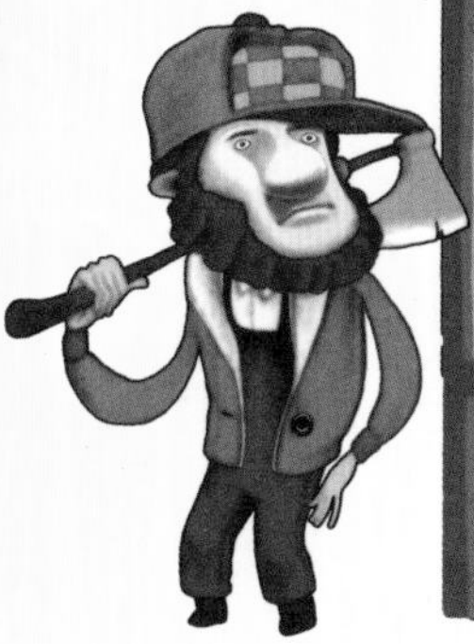

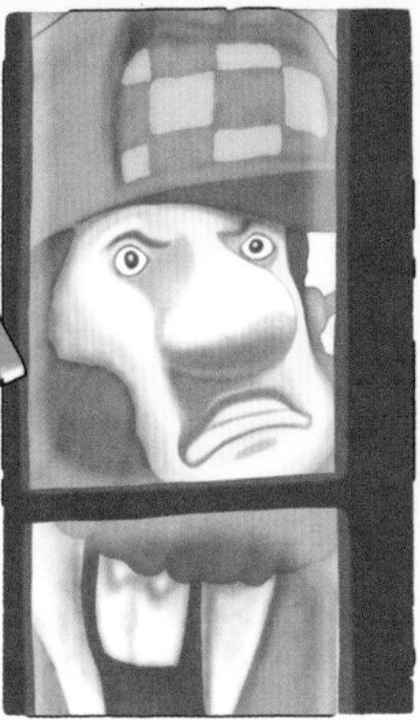

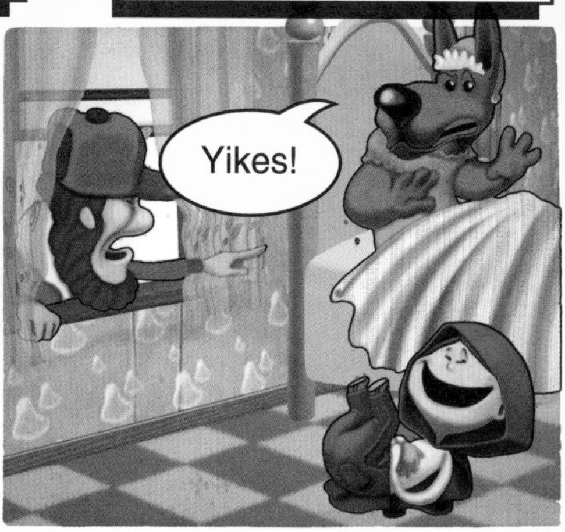
Yikes!

How embarrassing!

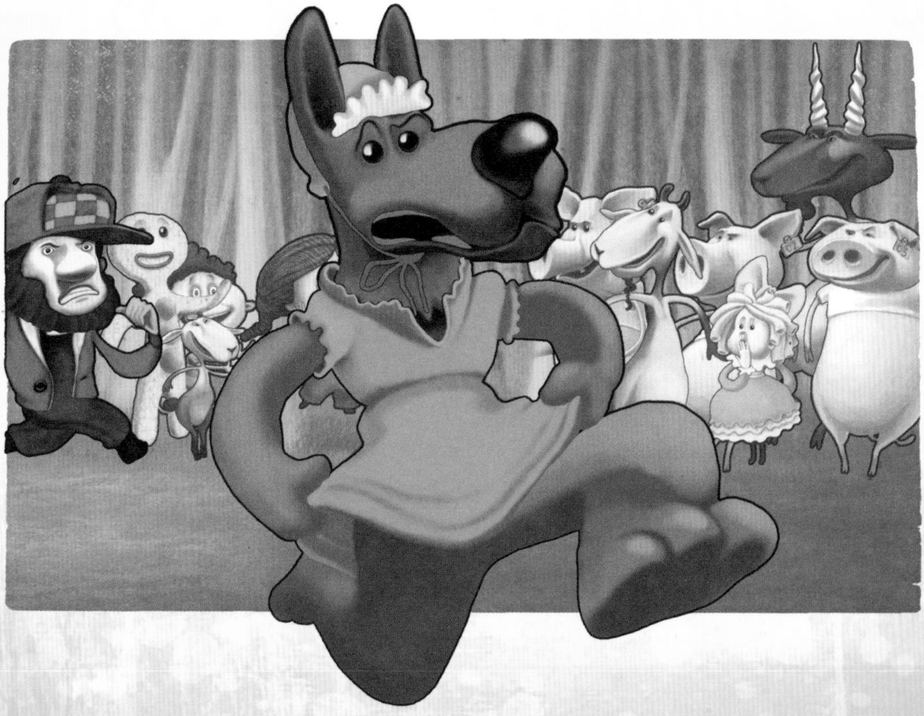

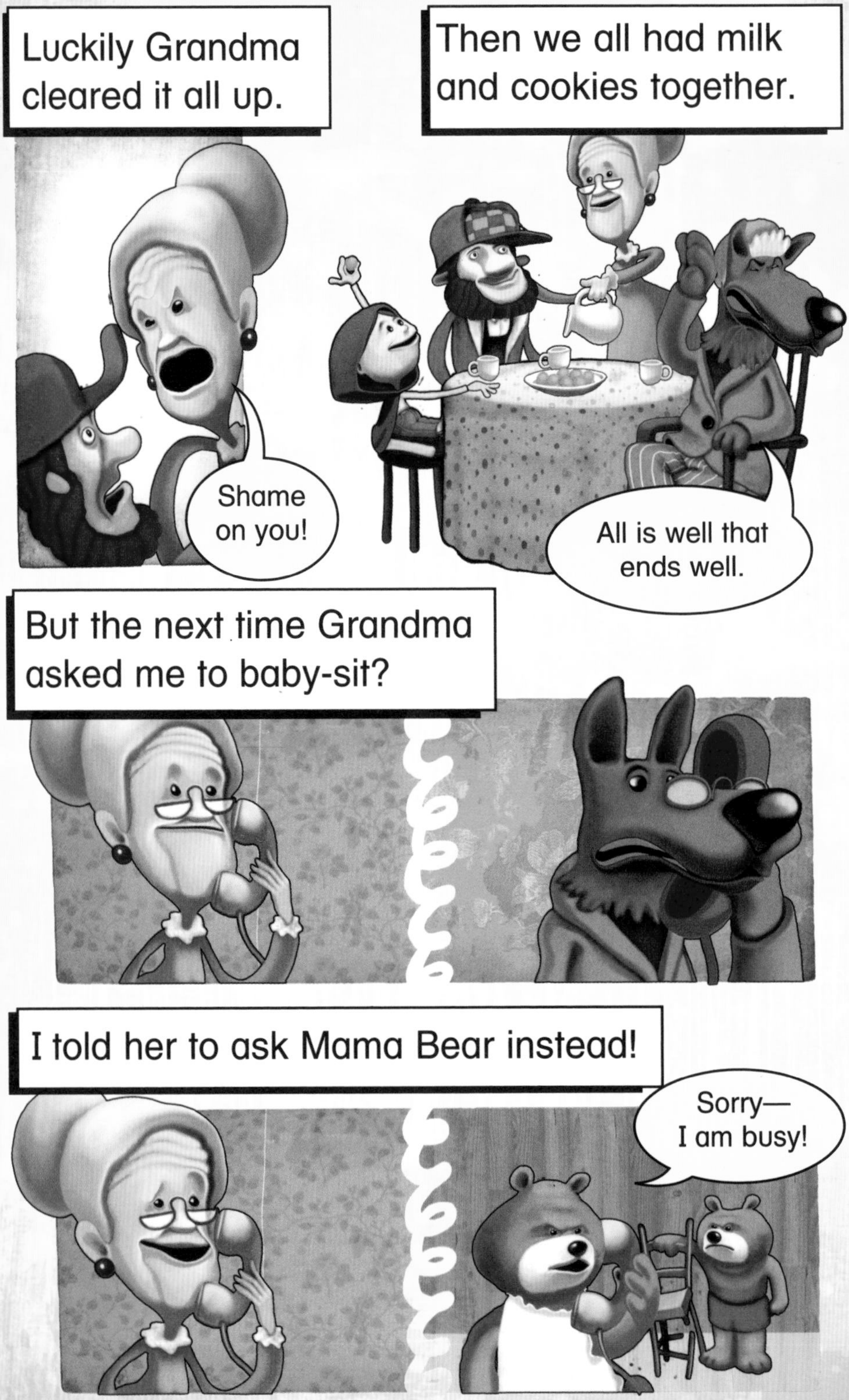
Luckily Grandma cleared it all up.
Shame on you!
Then we all had milk and cookies together.
All is well that ends well.
But the next time Grandma asked me to baby-sit?
I told her to ask Mama Bear instead!
Sorry—
I am busy!

THE GRASS IS ALWAYS GREENER

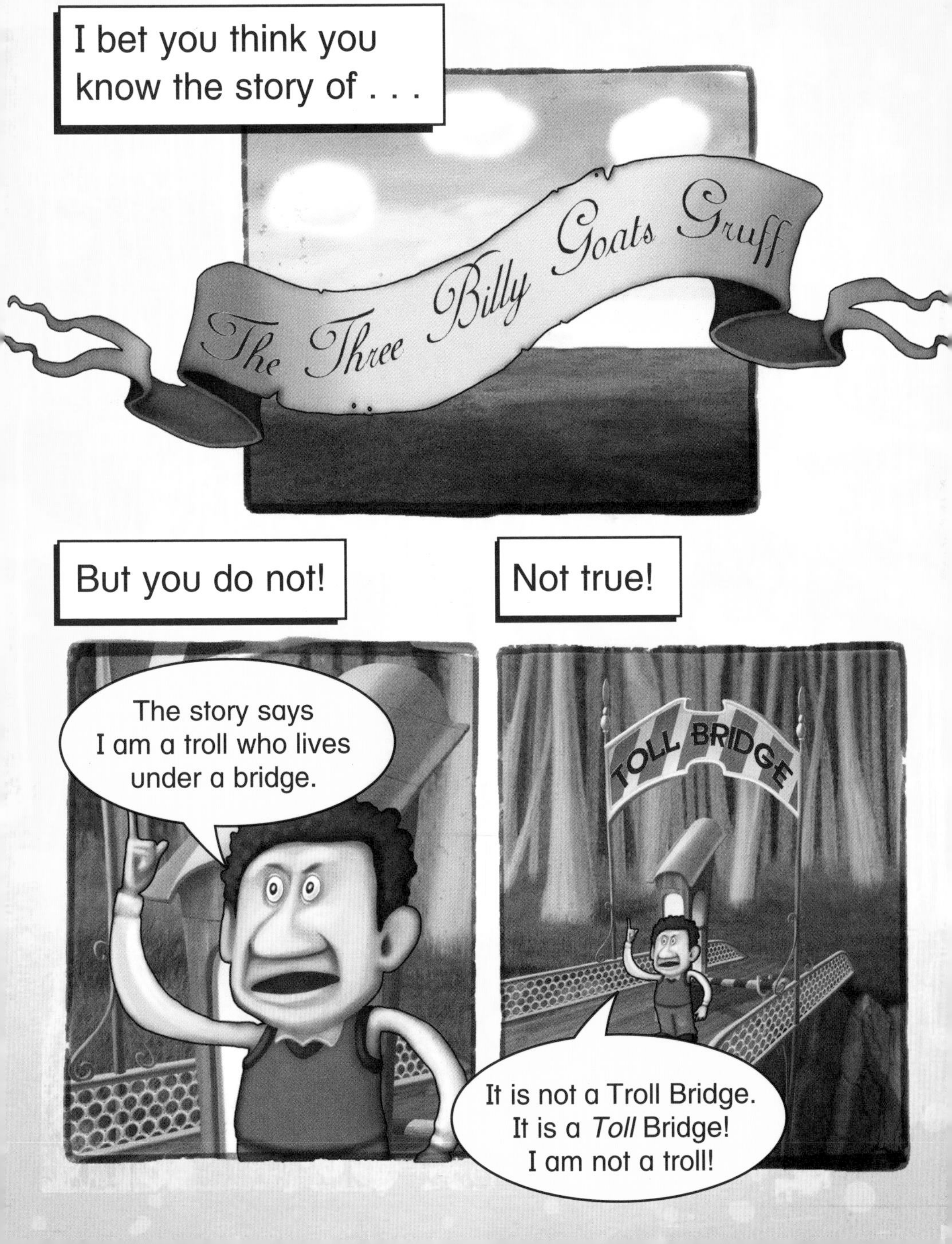
I bet you think you know the story of . . .
The Three Billy Goats Gruff
But you do not!
The story says I am a troll who lives under a bridge.
Not true!
TOLL BRIDGE
It is not a Troll Bridge. It is a *Toll* Bridge! I am not a troll!

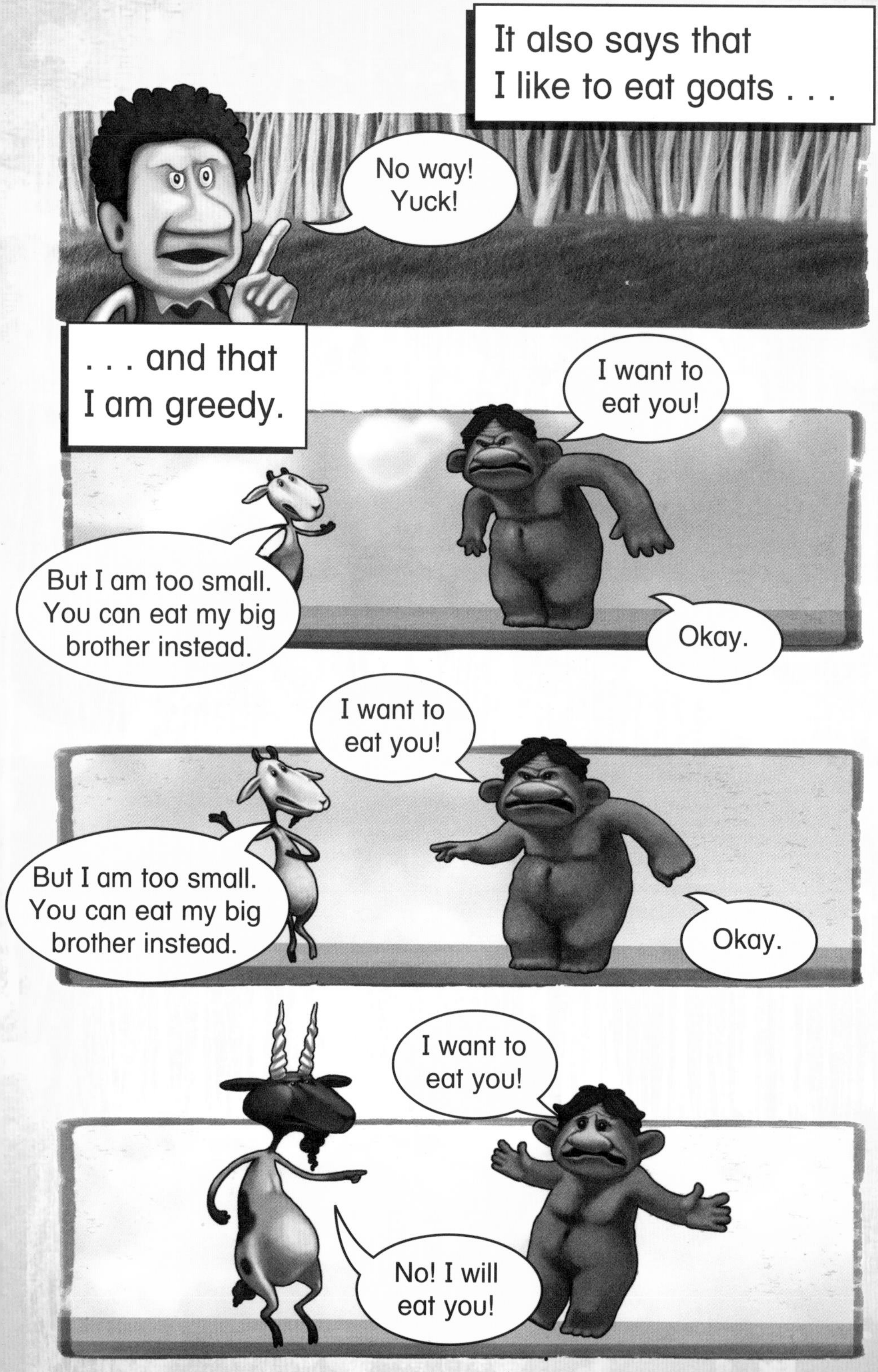
It also says that
I like to eat goats . . .
No way!
Yuck!
. . . and that
I am greedy.
I want to
eat you!
But I am too small.
You can eat my big
brother instead.
Okay.
I want to
eat you!
But I am too small.
You can eat my big
brother instead.
Okay.
I want to
eat you!
No! I will
eat you!

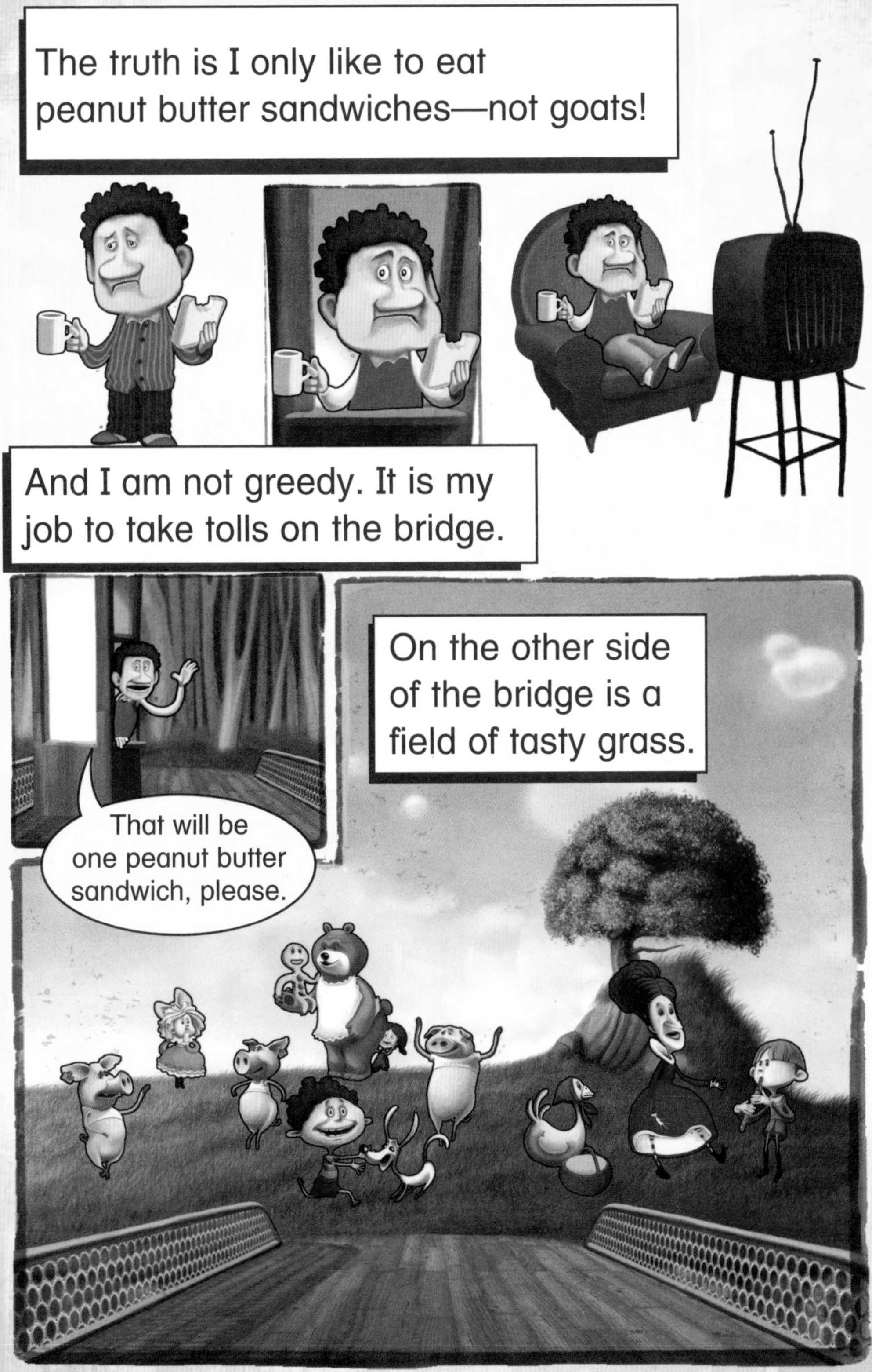
The truth is I only like to eat peanut butter sandwiches—not goats!
And I am not greedy. It is my job to take tolls on the bridge.
That will be one peanut butter sandwich, please.
On the other side of the bridge is a field of tasty grass.

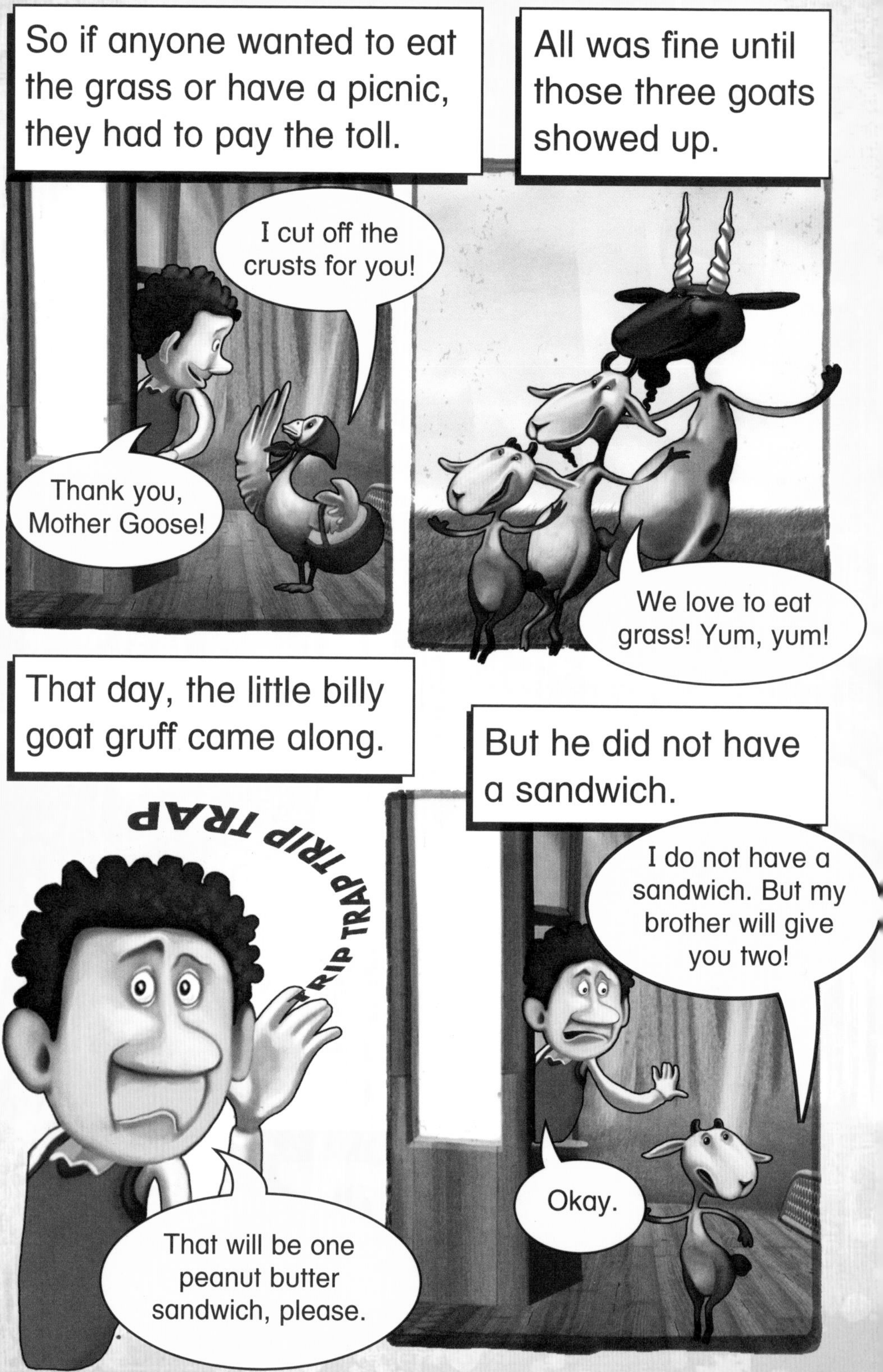
So if anyone wanted to eat the grass or have a picnic, they had to pay the toll.
I cut off the crusts for you!
Thank you, Mother Goose!
All was fine until those three goats showed up.
We love to eat grass! Yum, yum!
That day, the little billy goat gruff came along.
TRIP TRAP TRIP TRAP
That will be one peanut butter sandwich, please.
But he did not have a sandwich.
I do not have a sandwich. But my brother will give you two!
Okay.

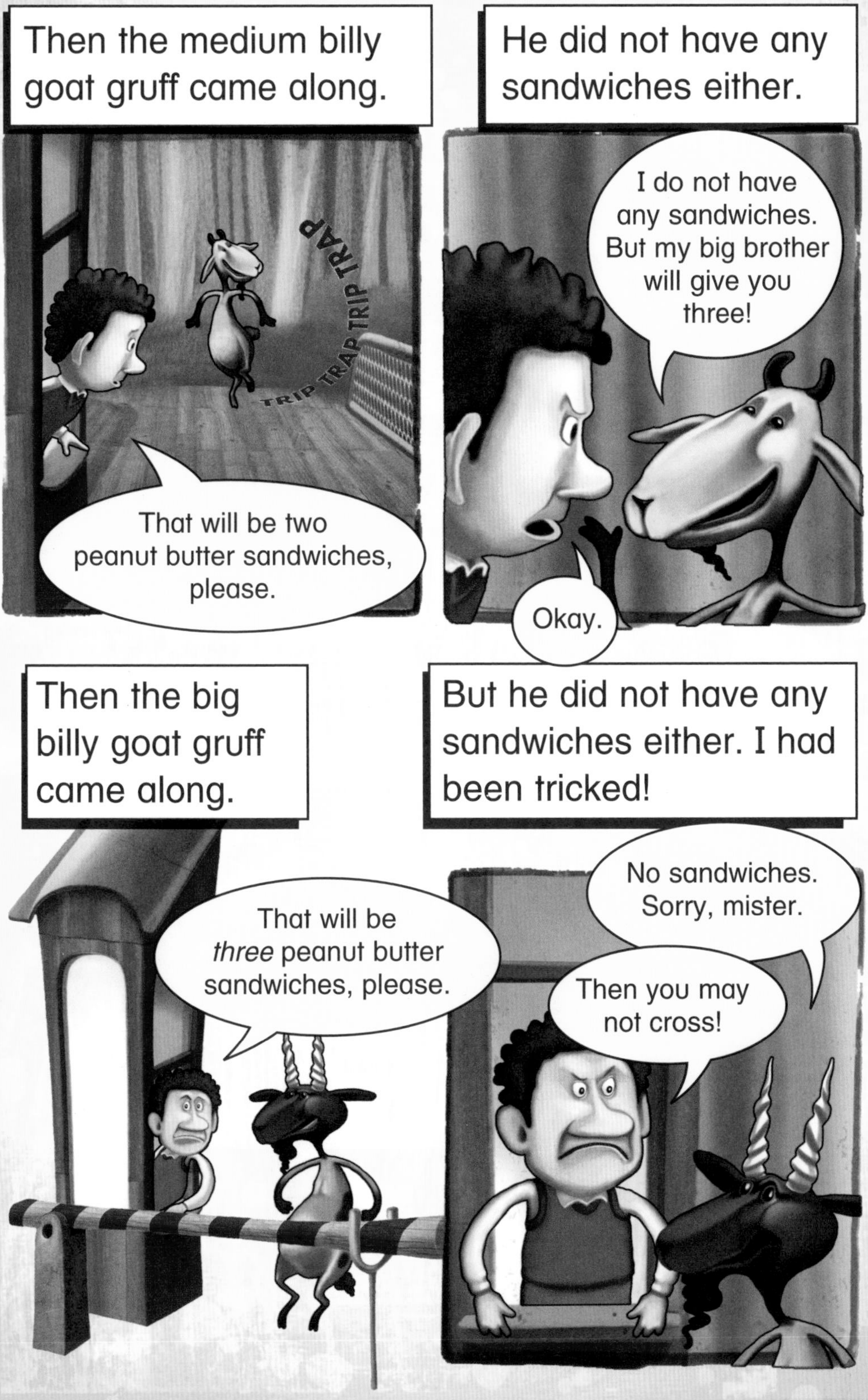
Then the medium billy goat gruff came along.
TRIP TRAP TRIP TRAP
That will be two peanut butter sandwiches, please.
He did not have any sandwiches either.
I do not have any sandwiches. But my big brother will give you three!
Okay.
Then the big billy goat gruff came along.
That will be *three* peanut butter sandwiches, please.
But he did not have any sandwiches either. I had been tricked!
No sandwiches. Sorry, mister.
Then you may not cross!

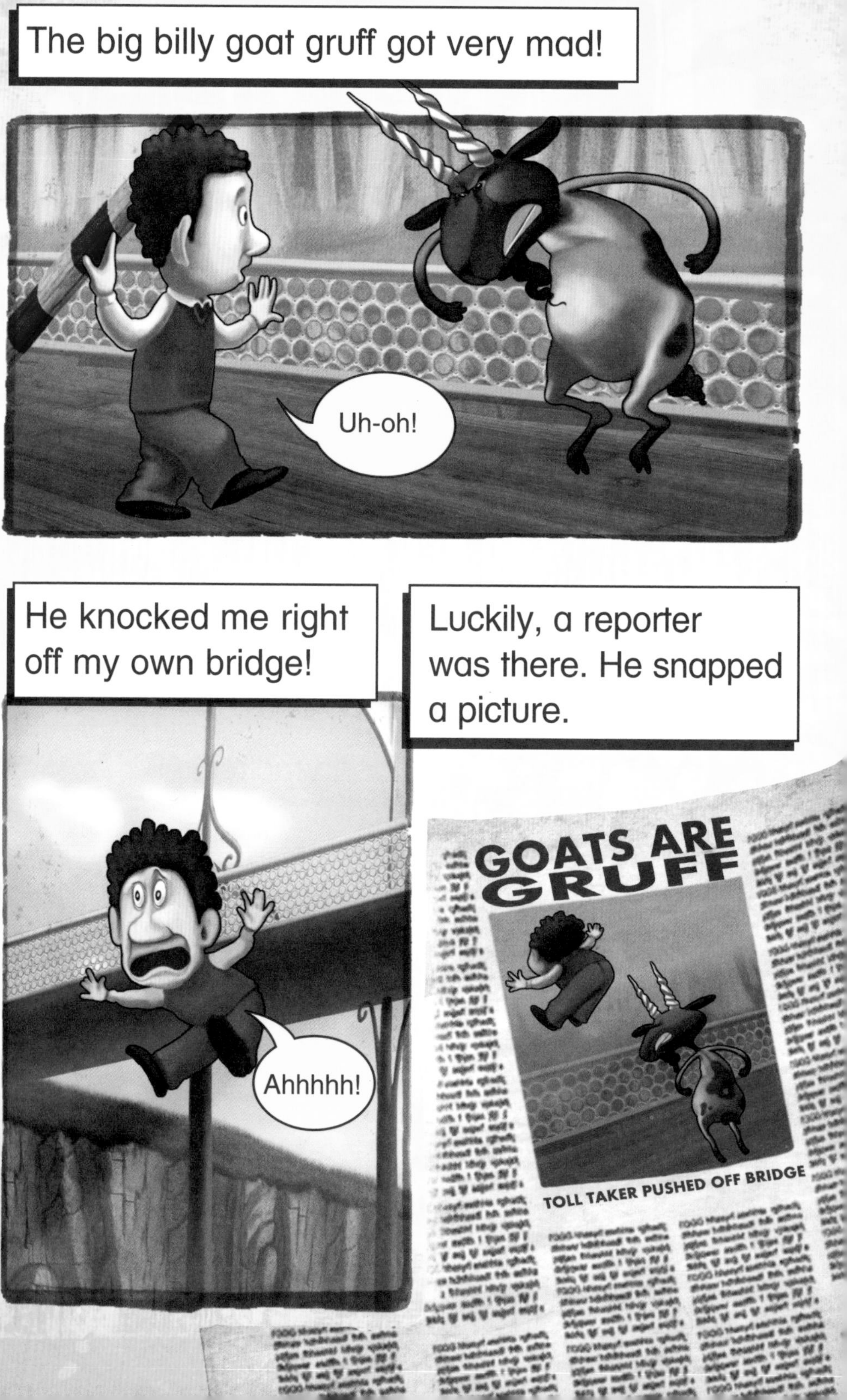

The big billy goat gruff got very mad!
Uh-oh!
He knocked me right off my own bridge!
Ahhhhh!
Luckily, a reporter was there. He snapped a picture.
GOATS ARE GRUFF
TOLL TAKER PUSHED OFF BRIDGE

When everyone saw it, they got mad.

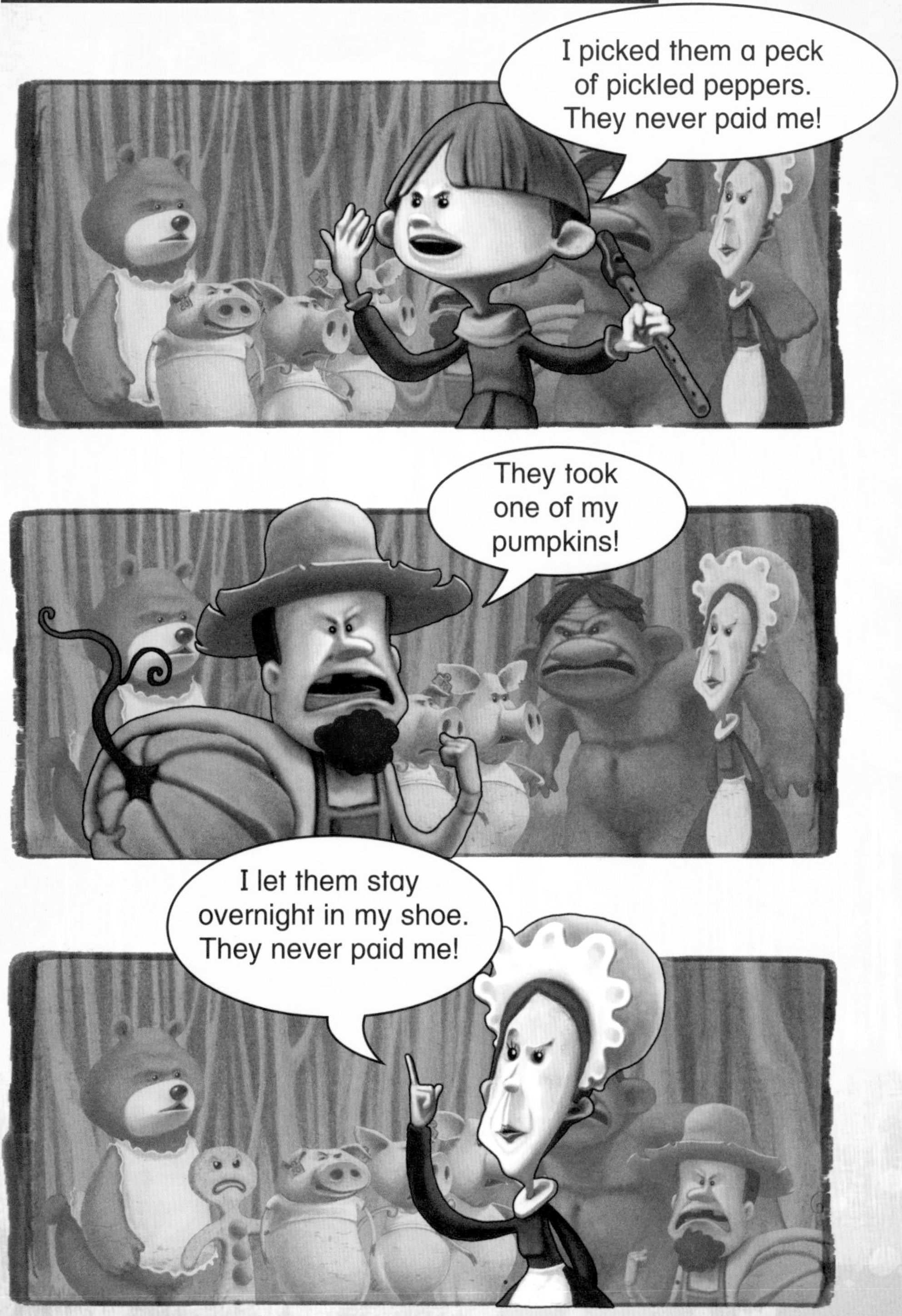
I picked them a peck of pickled peppers. They never paid me!
They took one of my pumpkins!
I let them stay overnight in my shoe. They never paid me!

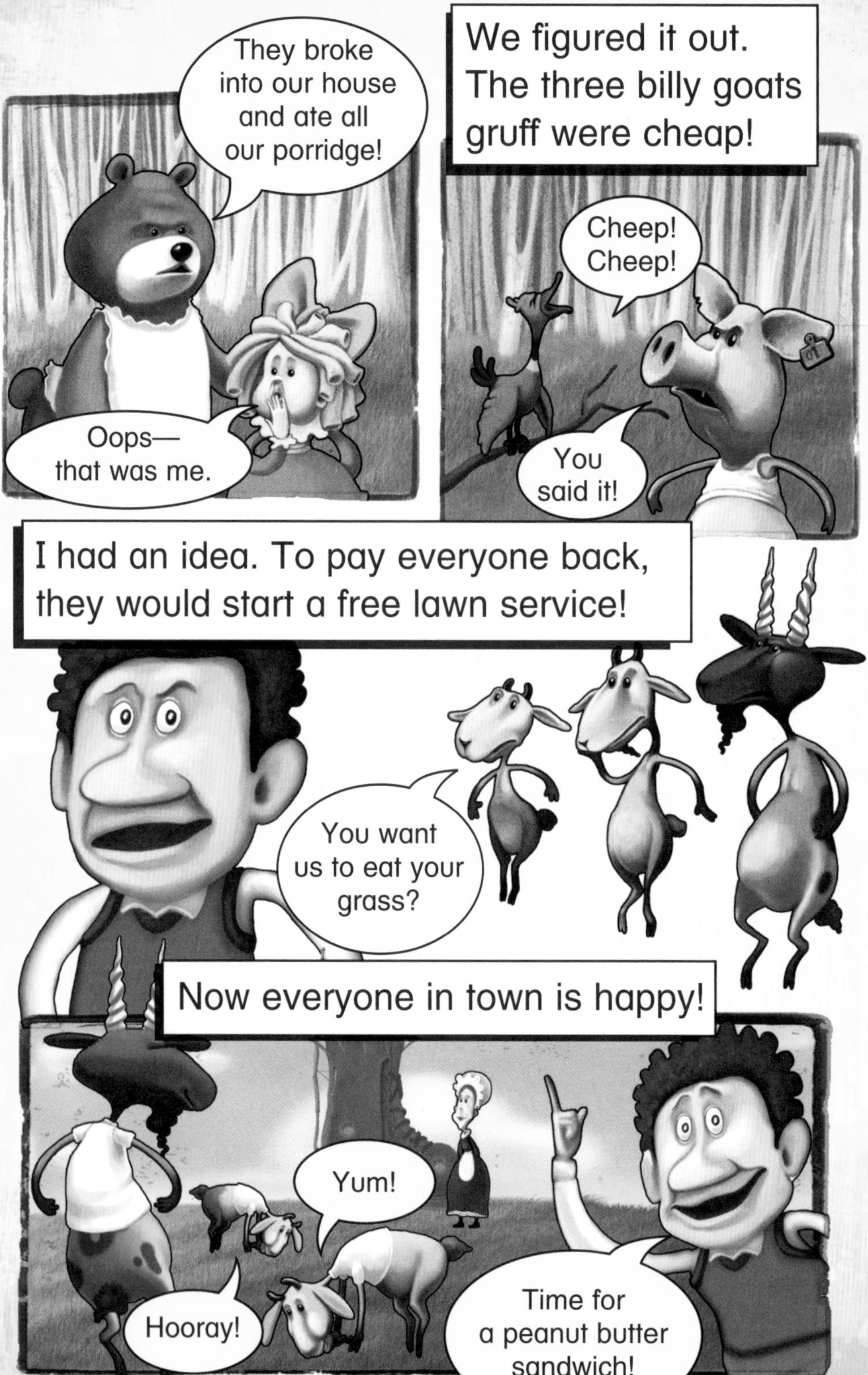
They broke into our house and ate all our porridge!
Oops— that was me.
We figured it out. The three billy goats gruff were cheap!
Cheep! Cheep!
You said it!
I had an idea. To pay everyone back, they would start a free lawn service!
You want us to eat your grass?
Now everyone in town is happy!
Yum!
Hooray!
Time for a peanut butter sandwich!